BOMBY
THE
BOMBARDIER
BEETLE

Author
Hazel May Rue

Project Director
Richard B. Bliss, Ed.D

Illustrator
Sandy Thornton

Institute for Creation Research
El Cajon, California

This Supplementary Material was developed as part of a
writing project by the Institute for Creation Research.

BOMBY, THE BOMBARDIER BEETLE

Published, produced and distributed by the **INSTITUTE for CREATION RESEARCH**

Richard B. Bliss, Ed.D., Project Director

CONSULTANTS

Theodore Fischbacher, Education, Ph.D.
Jean Sloat Morton, Biology, Ph.D.
Gary E. Parker, Biology, Ed.D.
Hazel May Rue, Education, M.S.
Harold S. Slusher, Physics, M.S., D.Sc., Ph.D.

CONTRIBUTING TEAM MEMBERS

ILLUSTRATORS

Shirlene Barrett, Jonathan Chong, Richard Holt, Doug Jennings, Karen Myers, Steve Pitstick, Marvin Ross, Barbara Sauer, Sandy Thornton, Linda Vance, Jay Wegter, Frankie Winn, Tim Lindquist, Ron Fisher, Jeanie Elliott

PROJECT WRITING STAFF

Deborah Bainer—Malaysia
Anne Beams—Germany
Gary G. Eastman—California
Elizabeth Ernst—Oregon
Kenneth F. Ernst, Jr.—Oregon
Olive Fischbacher—California
Norman Fox—Oregon
Virginia Gray Hastings—Illinois
Marilyn F. Hallman—Texas
Alberta Hanson—California
Deborah Hayes—Texas

Richard Holt— Iowa
Melody J. McIntyre—Pennsylvania
Fred Pauling—Virginia
Hazel May Rue—Oregon
Barbara Sauer—Illinois
Wilburn Sooter—Washington
Ivan Stonehocker—Canada
Harold C. Watkins—California
Susan E. Watkins—California
Fred Willson—California

BOMBY, THE BOMBARDIER BEETLE

Copyright© 1984

Third Printing, 1993

Institute for Creation Research
El Cajon, California 92021

Library of Congress Catalog Card Number

ISBN 0-932766-13-7

Cataloging in Publication Data

Bomby, the bombardier beetle / Hazel Mae Rue ; Sandy Thornton, ill.

1. Bombardier beetle. I. Title.
II. Series.

595.76

ISBN 0-932766-13-7   82-71053

Introduction to the Student

Dear Student,

The purpose of this book is, first of all, that you may enjoy meeting this family of **bombardier beetles**. **Bomby**, like all of the young, wants to learn all he can about himself and the world in which he lives.

Second, you will learn about other beetles and other **insects**. Insects of all kinds are very important to us and to our **environment**. We are likely to hear more about the beetles that are harmful to us, to our crops, and to our forests. There are 290,000 described **species** in the world and more are being identified and cataloged each year. Insects are the most numerous of all **earth**'s **creatures** and the beetles are the numerical champions. One of every five living creatures is a beetle, and they vary in size from one-hundredth of an inch to the African goliath which measures four inches in length.

Third, perhaps you want to learn to think, search, and research. Keep your eyes and ears open. Keep your mind open. You may want to become an **entomologist** and make an in-depth study of these little creatures. You may wonder what purpose God had in creating this little beetle in the first place. As you read further about Bomby and his interesting ways, you are sure to be amazed at the creative genius of our Creator.

Some words may be new to you. If a word is in blacker letters (like some of the words on this page) you can look up what it means in the Glossary in the back of the book.

The Author

Table of Contents

Bomby listens

Chapter 1
Under the Stone

"Bomby, Bomby," called Mother. "Now that you are almost a full-grown Bombardier Beetle, go over there to your father. Find out what you are supposed to know in order to live on this earth. Learn to take care of yourself. Learn how a Bombardier Beetle is supposed to behave."

Mother was giving directions to the youngest **member** of her family. Of course, you and I as people would have heard absolutely nothing.

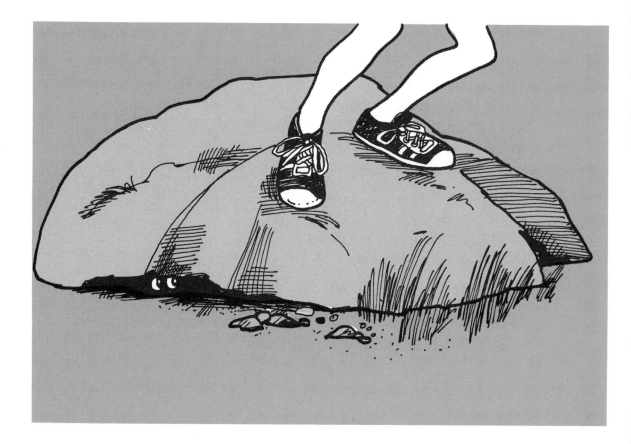

This family of beetles lived under a large rock that was so heavy no snoopy child could lift it up. Many beetle families are not as **wise** as the special family we are getting to know. They choose smaller stones or even a **plank** under which to live. A child can lift their stones and peek at them. Then everyone in the family has to run for his life. Sometimes a brave Uncle or Grandfather would fire his **cannons**. Wait, let's not get ahead of the tales Father has to tell Bomby.

Bomby went slowly to Father who was **munching** on a tidbit. Bomby took a piece of his lunch and started to munch, too.

"Well, Bomby, it is time for you to learn the ways of our family," Father started his **story**. "In the very first place, we are the largest family on earth. One in every five living creatures is a beetle. We got our name, *Bombardier Beetles*, from the cannons in our tail end. Our family's **scientific** name is **carabids** of the **Brachinus genus**. Men have guns and bombs to fight and protect themselves. We were created with cannons for our protection. Actually, people can learn much from us. If you expect to live a long life and to be as wise as Great, Great, Great, ever and ever so Great Great-grandfather Bomb..."

"What is so great about Grandfather Bomb?" Bomby started to ask.

OUR FAMILY'S SCIENTIFIC NAME IS 'CARABIDS OF THE BRACHINUS GENUS.'

"That just means that he is my father's, father's, father's—hey, never mind about that. Keep still and **listen**. He is very old and very wise. When he was young, he listened. He learned how to take care of himself and his family. That is why we are here."

Bomby hung his head. He even stopped **chewing** for a second or two.

"I want to be wise," he said. He wanted to ask what wise meant. What did it have to do with living a long time? He knew if he wanted to be wise—whatever it meant—he had better listen and listen well.

Father stopped chewing for a second. "The word beetle comes from an old **English** word. People don't even use it anymore. The word is '**bitan**.' It used to mean 'bite.' We bite and chew so they call us beetles. We can't suck plant **juice**. We can't sip **nectar**, but boy, oh boy—can we bite and chew!" He began to chew harder than ever.

Bomby wanted to ask, "What are people?" He stopped and thought. "If I'm to learn anything, I have to keep still and listen. Of course, I can bite and chew. All beetles bite and chew." He took a bite of lunch and chewed and chewed.

Chapter 2
Poison Gas Specialist

"We are a wise *Bombardier Beetle* family," Father began again. "We live under a big, heavy boulder (a great, great big rock). No person can lift it up and bother us. I hope people never take a **machine** and turn our boulder over."

Bomby looked up at the cool, dark boulder over his head and was glad he belonged to a wise family whatever "wise" meant.

11

"We are the first **poison** gas **specialists**!" Father **continued**. People want to be wise. They study us and learn our ways. We have two little **exhaust valves** on our tail end."

Bomby twisted and turned as he tried to see his tail pipes. He couldn't see behind himself. Father was talking. Bomby knew he had better listen for all he was worth if he wanted to live and be wise.

"As I was saying," Father continued, "some people get too close to us, then we have to use our poison gas to **scare** them away. When we want to scare away a person—a person is one people—we just fire away at them. They can't believe we know how to use chemicals through our tail pipes. People were on earth a long time before they knew how to use **chemicals**. God created us this way in the beginning."

"People—people are awkward creatures—great **huge** things that clump, clump, clump all over the earth. People are our worst enemies. They don't mean to be our **enemies**. They just tear up our ground."

"People don't really mean to hurt us. We are useful to them. We kill many insects that eat their crops. Crops are their food. People are always tearing up the ground...building things, making **canals**, making roads. Sometimes, they stumble over a stone and take the roof off our house. Next time, I'll tell you about our other enemies." Bomby wanted to ask more about the enemies now, but he knew he had better wait.

Chapter 3
Listen, Bomby

Time came for another story. It was really a lesson. Father made the lesson very interesting. The lesson was just a good story.

"Now listen to this, Bomby. One very **danger**ous enemy is the **Tiger** Beetle. He is really out to get us."

Bomby moved a little closer to Father. Father continued. "The Tiger Beetle is metallic blue, green, purple, or orange. He is about our size. He is a **fierce** creature. He is very active. He can move fast. We have one up on him though! Hear this . . . I was walking along minding my own **business**. I was enjoying the bright moonlight one spring evening. Out of my left eye I saw this TB coming. TB means Tiger Beetle, of course. He was sneaking up on me from behind and coming fast . . . I didn't let on I saw him. He was just ready to grab me. I let go with both **barrels** of poison gas. That stopped him in his tracks. He was dazed. I could see he was dizzy. He turned around and got out of there in a hurry."

"When we go out you must stay near me or near some stones. Soon you will know how to scare Tiger Beetles, too. I am glad, Bomby, that you know enough to listen. I see that you want to ask **questions**, but you haven't. You will know what I am talking about if you listen. Have you found out what you wanted to know?"

"Well, yes, Father. I know what people are and what a person is. If I listen a lot, I'll be wise, won't I?"

"Yes, you will. I think you take after your Great, Great, Great, ever and ever so Great Great-Grand-father Bomb—the Bombardier Beetle."

"I never took after anyone," Bomby thought. "I would like to know how I got here on this earth. What is 'the earth'? Where did I come from? I won't ask. I will keep still and listen and listen."

"I must tend to my chewing now. Some other time I will tell you more." Father went out to hunt for something to chew.

Bomby went out to play. He played near some stones. He tried to tell one of his **friends** what he had learned from his father. His friend asked one silly question after another.

Bomby gave up trying to talk. He said to his friend, "Go ask your Father!"

Bomby was sad

Chapter 4
A Sad Story

Bomby settled down close to his father to hear more about life.

Father was chewing and chewing. Bomby started to chew, too. Father started to talk. Bomby listened very hard and tried to chew quietly.

"Keep on chewing, Bomby," his father said. "We make our poison chemicals from amino acids. **Amino acids** are the 'building blocks' of food called **protein**. Every creature needs protein to live. We need protein to live. We need even more protein to make our poison chemicals.

"Another enemy that we have is the ant. They sometimes attack us in groups. Sometimes there is a whole **army** of ants. We can hold our own and drive them off by shooting time after time. We can shoot over a thousand times real fast if we have to."

"A frog is a big animal that may attack us. A frog gets away fast when we shoot poison spray in his face."

Father had been chewing all the time he was talking to Bomby. Now he took another bite. Bomby waited. He wanted very much to be a wise Bombardier Beetle. Soon Father went on.

"I have a sad story that I must tell you, Bomby." "Go ahead and tell me. I won't cry. I want to learn and be wise," Bomby said. He chewed slowly and thoughtfully.

Father sighed a beetlish sigh. He talked slowly.

"We can handle Tiger Beetles. We can drive away armies of ants. Big frogs back away from our poison gas. Even people leave us alone."

"However, there are some species of **orb-weaving spiders** for which we must watch out. They are a common variety. As you know, we can fly. We don't fly very often. If a Bombardier Beetle flies into this spider's web he lands in a soft silken cradle. He isn't afraid. The spider comes quietly. He **wraps** soft, silken **threads** around the Bombardier Beetle. All of a sudden the spider bites. The Bombardier Beetle tries to fire his cannons. Too bad! The cannons won't work. The cannons are closed and wrapped tightly in soft, silken webbing. The spider has a good dinner."

"Oh, Father! How terrible! If I ever land in a soft, silken web, I won't wait. I will fire all of the rounds of chemical ammunition I have."

"I wish you well, Bomby," said Father Bombardier Beetle. "I wish you well, but look where you are going and don't get caught."

Chapter 5
Cousin Bo Goes Under

Bomby saw that Father was settled down munching on tidbits again. He thought that he would go over near him and just listen. He hoped that Father would start talking. Bomby was still wondering how he ever got on this earth and what "the earth" is.

"Okay, Bomby, I suppose you want to know how you got here."

"Yes, Father, I do, but I am not asking, I am listening."

"Well, well, long ago I saw this nice looking girl bombardier beetle. Her name was **Diery**, but I hadn't met her yet."

"That is Mother's name," yelled Bomby–and then he remembered! He got very quiet, except for chewing. He chewed for dear life!

"My **cousin**, Bo, took a liking to Diery, but she wouldn't even look at him. Bo kept going over to her. She would walk away. He would follow her. He got bolder. Then he got bolder. Diery just took off running as fast as she could go. Cousin Bo ran after her. He got close behind her. She stopped. She let him have it right in the face with both cannons.

Well, that stopped him!

Female Bombardier Beetles have a slightly different poison gas from ours. The male can't stand to have it fired in his face. Bo had had it! He  **staggered** and weaved from side to side. He rolled over on his back. I thought that he was dead. His legs were stiff. He lay on his back for about three hours.

"Then I saw him move a little. Once he started to move, he got better quickly. In thirty minutes he got to his feet. He ran away. I thought Diery showed that she was a very wise Lady Bombardier Beetle. I thought she would make a good mother for my **children.** I went over to her. She seemed to like me. We became friends. Then we thought we would become a pair and raise a family. Diery laid some eggs. She was ready to spray with her poison gas any male beetle that came to eat them. A beetle egg turns into a larva. We generally call them 'grubs.' The larva or grub grows up to be a **pupa**, and finally a Bombardier Beetle—and here you are!"

"One of every five creatures on the earth is some sort of beetle. Right, Father?"

"Right you are, Bomby. It pays to listen. You are learning. I think you will be wise. If you learn to look and listen, you may live a long while. Go out and play now. Stay close to home and watch out for Tiger Beetles.

Hydroquinone and hydrogen peroxide

Inner chamber

Outer chamber

Quinone spray

Two-chambered glands

Chapter 6
Bomby Learns Defense

"Now it is time for you to hear more about our way of defending ourselves in case we can't outrun the enemy. As you know, we have these two tail pipes. You can plainly see them. We have two **glands** in our tail ends. One makes '**hydroquinone**.' The other makes '**hydrogen peroxide**.' These two go together into a 'collecting room.' There is another room called a 'firing **chamber**.' In there is a mixture of from 40% to 60% **solution** made of **catalase** and **peroxidase**. This solution comes out of the walls of the firing chamber. The muscle shoots the first two liquids out through the firing chamber. It keeps right on going and **explodes** outside of our tail pipes. If it exploded inside, it would blow any Bombardier Beetle to **smithereens**. No beetle has ever been blown up." Bomby thanked God for such a perfect design.

"Come out for a walk. It is dark now and I want you to see for yourself how this works."

Bomby and
Father crawled
out from under the
protection of their
boulder into the dark
night. Bomby hoped
there were no Tiger
Beetles waiting for them. All
was quiet. It was a warm, dark
night. The stars twinkled far
away. There was no moon in sight. Father walked
ahead of Bomby.

"Don't get too close to me, Bomby. I am going to
pretend that there is a Tiger Beetle coming, and I am
going to fire away at him." Bomby dropped farther
behind, but when Father fired both barrels, Bomby
jumped a whole inch into the air.

"Father, Father! Are you all right?" screamed Bomby.

"Sh-sh-sh. Be quiet, Bomby. Of course, I'm all
right."

"Oh, Father, what a smell. Yuk! There was a big
flash of light. There was a big bang. I felt heat! My, it
was hot! I am glad I was back a long way. If I had
been closer, I would have been scared stiff."

"It was hot," Father said. "It was 100' **Celsius** or
212' **Fahrenheit**. Water will boil at 212' Fahrenheit.
Bomby, you wouldn't have been scared stiff, but it
would have been mighty unpleasant! Male Bombardier
Beetles learn from their fathers and female Bombardier
Beetles learn from their mothers. If your mother fired at
you, then you would have been 'scared stiff' for sure.
You would be dizzy and faint. You would have rolled
over on your back and gotten stiff all over. You would
have stayed that way for two or three hours.

24

Then you would have awakened and been all right. That was what happened to my cousin, Bo, when your mother fired at him. The female Bombardier Beetles are not affected by the explosion from their mothers. You are not **affected** by an explosion from me. It isn't pleasant, but you don't pass out."

"It isn't pleasant! That is for sure. Please don't ever do that to me again."

"Oh, I will never do it again. We only fire when in danger. Of course, we must **teach** our young Bombardier Beetles about life. God gave us this defense mechanism to use wisely."

"Can I do it **once**, Father? Please, please....," begged Bomby.

"Yes, just once. Remember, we don't fire unless there is danger. Walk ahead of me now—hurry up, get way ahead. Did you see a cloud of smoke-like vapor when I fired?"

"No" answered Bomby. "I just saw a flash of light."

"There was a cloud of vapor at the same time," Father said. As Bomby walked ahead he looked from side to side. He hoped he wouldn't see a Tiger Beetle.

"Bomby, Bomby! Fire your cannon! Fire your cannon!" yelled Father.

Bomby was scared. He thought a Tiger Beetle was coming. He let go with both barrels. Bang! Bang! He was really scared. He thought his father had sounded scared, too.

HEY, I DID IT!

25

"Very good, Bomby. That would have scared off a Tiger Beetle. Even a 'person' would have gotten away from you. There was a big flash. I heard a loud bang. Whew, there was a bad smell and a fine cloud of vapor! You did very well."

"I thought there was a Tiger Beetle coming after me. You sounded scared, Father."

"Bombardier Beetles can't fire unless they think there is danger. I wanted you to fire really well. You did, Bomby. I'm proud of you."

"Were you really scared when you fired to show me how?" Bomby asked.

"I let myself remember very clearly how the Tiger Beetle looked when he nearly got me. I could almost see him coming—so I fired away. I hope you will always remember to thank our Creator for our defense mechanism Bomby."

All at once Father moved very quickly. He grabbed a night **insect.**

"Every family has some foolish members," he said.

"The one I caught was not wise. I caught a foolish one. It will taste good. Let us drag it closer to our boulder and eat it." So they had an **evening** snack. My, my, how they did bite and chew and chew and bite.

26

Chapter 7
Great-ever-so-Great-grandfather

"Bomby, you are nearly grown up. Soon you will be wise enough to be on your own and start your own family. There are more lessons that you need to learn. These lessons you will get from your great, great, great, ever and ever so great, great-grandfather. Now you know enough to keep still and listen. I will listen, too. I want to hear *The* **Stories** one more time. Soon it will be my turn to tell them to the young Bombardier Beetles."

"Come with me, Bomby."

Father and Bomby made their way to a very dark corner under some stones. There they found the wisest of all Bombardier Beetles. He was **dozing** away and chewing slowly on a tidbit.

"Hello, Great-grandfather Bomb, said Father. "I have with me young Bomby who wants to hear *The Stories* from you."

"Can't you tell *The Stories* yourself, yet? You have heard them over and over. It is a good thing I am wise. I take good care of myself. I am so very old and so very wise. You young beetles don't take **responsibilities**!" He glared at Father.

Bomby was afraid that Father would get mad and fire away at Grandfather for calling him a "young beetle."

Father only hung his head and said, "No one can ever tell *The Stories* as well as you tell them. I want to hear them one more time."

"Grandfather began to look pleased, but he mumbled, "One more time. One more time. I have heard that many times before. I will tell them one more time. Here is Story Number One as it was told to me when I was young by my great, great, great, great ever and ever so great great-grandfather as it was told to him by his great, great . . ."

"Yes, Grandfather, go on with *The Story*," father said gently.

"Well, it all happened a long time ago. Even **according** to people it was a long time ago. Thousands of years ago."

Bomby hears about God's plan

"Yes, Grandfather, it was long ago. Go on with *The Story*." Father reminded him.

"Yes, yes," said Grandfather. "This is what I remember from my Grandfather, Bomby." He said: "God created all kinds of life. God told us about this in a book called the Bible. He even told us that we were created on the sixth day of creation."

Bomby thought about all of this very carefully. "Actually, this makes me something very special," he thought. Bomby knew that he would have to talk some more about this with Grandfather.

Grandfather had a far away look in his eyes. Then he asked, "Bomby, have you ever seen sap from a tree?"

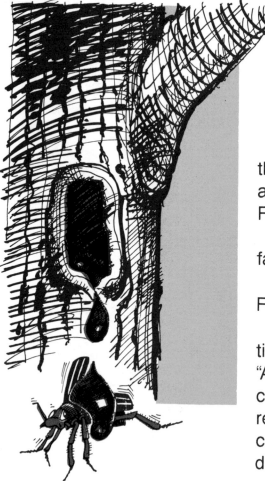

Bomby looked at his father and back to his grandfather. Then he shook his head.

"You tell your story, Grandfather, and I'll **explain** the part about the **fossil resin** and show him some sap," Father said, looking at Bomby.

"Long, long, long..." Grandfather began.

"Go on with the story," - Father said to him.

Grandfather chewed three times. Then he continued. "A Bombardier Beetle got close to a tree. The sap, or resin as it is sometimes called, was drip, drip, drip, drip, dripping."

"What happened then, Grandfather?" Father asked.

"Well, the Beetle almost stepped into the sticky mess. Then he started to fly. Up he went. Up, up, up-then pow! Something hit him in midair! His wings closed. He was caught in a round drop of resin as it fell. That was the end of him! Some people found him a long, long, long...."

"Yes, Grandfather, people found him after the resin was **petrified**. The first Bombardier Beetle ever found was in petrified resin. Petrified resin is called **amber**. People think it is very beautiful.

Grandfather nodded, "Yes, that's the way it was. Come back tomorrow and I'll tell you some more. Now I must chew, and doze, and dream."

Father whispered, "Thank you, Grandfather," as he and Bomby went quietly away.

Chapter 8
Dragons & Beetles

"Bomby," Father said, "Let us go and see Grand-father. He will tell us more about our past." They went to see Grandfather, who was chewing in his dark corner.

"Hello, Grandfather. Bomby and I want to hear a story."

Grandfather took a big bite as he greeted them.

"Now I will tell you more about our past."

"Now you remember what I told you about our creation Bomby, don't you?"

"I remember that you said God created us and that there was a story about this in the Bible; but tell me more," urged Bomby.

"Well, son, you sure have a good memory, but I will tell you even more exciting things. Our Creator created many things. He created other beetles, even the Tiger Beetle that we fear so much. He created humans, dogs, frogs and many other things. Isn't it nice to know that you are part of God's big plan?"

"It sure is Grandfather, now, I understand why I am made so wonderfully."

"We got the name *Bombardier Beetle* because we have this special little cannon on our tail end. Now hear this one! Some even think that great serpents once lived that breathed out fire from their mouth. When they sneezed there was such a shower of fire as hasn't been seen since that long, long, long...."

"Come on, Great-grandfather–that long ago day when the earth was very young."

"Oh, where was I?" Grandfather asked himself.

"Oh, yes, these serpents were huge and I mean huge. They had a firing **system** like ours–oh, I said that. Their firing systems were said to have been really huge. They were good at firing their cannons. They were very fierce. All the people on the earth were afraid of them. They stayed as far away as they could get. In some **countries** the people called them dragons. Some brave **knights** lived to tell their children about **dragons**. Their children's, children's, children's. . ."

"Yes, Grandfather, their children's, children's, children called them fairy tales. They liked to hear them, but they didn't believe them."

"Yes," said Grandfather, "that is what happened. Dragons weren't wise at all. They became **extinct**. However, we handled our cannons much better than the dragons did. Of course, we are so very, very, very, very...."

"Yes, Grandfather, we are very little and people aren't really afraid of us, but they do treat us with re-spect!"

"Oh, let me tell you something very funny. Once when I was young a long, long, long, long, long..."

"Yes, Grandfather, what funny thing happened long, long ago?" Father wanted to hear this.

"Well, I was out walking one evening while it was still light. A little child saw me. She picked me up—as **tiny** children will do. She started to put me into her mouth. Well, I couldn't let that happen! When she got me to her mouth, I let go with both barrels. She threw me into the air. She let out a scream. Her mother and father and all the neighbors came running. My, such a fuss. I landed on all six legs and ran for some rocks as fast as I could go. I got under one and peeked out. The people couldn't tell what happened. The little child couldn't talk. She just grabbed at her mouth and **howled**. Her mother looked down her throat. She washed her mouth with soap and water."

"That child grew up to be one of the people who are 'scared to death' of all creeping things. Now you two go on about your business and let me chew and dream about when I was young."

"Thank you, Grand-father," said Bomby. He felt very wise.

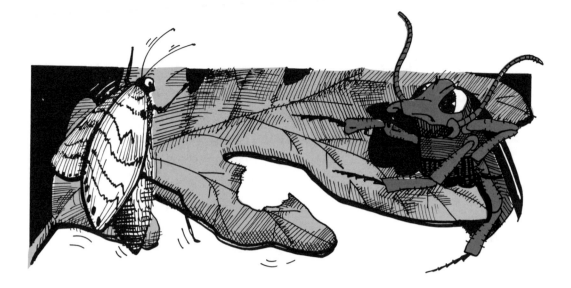

"Thank you, Grandfather," said Father. He knew that soon he would be the one to tell *The Story.* Bomby and his father went away and left Grandfather Bomb to his dreams.

"We are a big family and a very important family, aren't we, Father?" Bomby wanted to know.
"Yes," said Father, "People learn a lot from us. Part of the wing on their airplane gets it's name from our wing. Our hard outer wing is called on **elytron**. Our two wings together make an **elytra**."

"Beetles are very important. One branch of our family called the European **Calosoma** beetle was brought to the United States to help get rid of the gypsy moth. Gypsy moths eat the leaves of plants and trees that people need.

"Ha," said Father, "Even a reptile or a bird will spit out a Bombardier Beetle once it gets a taste of our poison gas. Soldiers on horses use a rifle with a short barrel. It sounds like a Bombardier Beetle when it fires. The rifle is much, much louder than a Bombardier Beetle's very loudest blast."

"Thank you, Father, for teaching me. I will keep learning. I will think as best as a Bombardier Beetle can think. I want to be as wise as you and Great, Great, Great, ever and ever so Great-grandfather are." Bomby thought again about his wise Creator.

"You can listen. You will be wise," Father said. Bomby silently thought again about his wise Creator.

Bomby and Father found a cool place under their boulder to have lunch and they chewed and chewed and chewed. Bomby asked his father to tell him more about the Bible and creation.

Pronunciation Key

The following pronunciation key is based on the Thorndike-Barnhart School Dictionary. These markings are used in your margin glossary to help you pronounce important words.

hat, āge, fär

let, ēqual, térm

it, īce

hot, ōpen, ôrder, oil, out

cup, put, rüle

ch, child

ng, long

sh, she

th, thin

Ŧh, then

zh, measure

uh represents *a* in about, *e* in taken, *i* in pencil,
  o in lemon, *u* in circus

Glossary

according	uh kor′ ding	in agreement with
acids	as′ idz	sour, tart
affected	uh fek′ tid	acted upon, influenced
amber	am′ buhr	yellowish fossil resin
amino	uh mē′ nō	compounds mixed to make protein
army	är′ mē	organized soldiers
barrels	bar′ uhlz	round containers with flat ends
beetle	bē′ tuhl	insect with hard shell-like wings
bitan	bīt′ uhn	to bite (Old English)
boil	boil	liquids bubble up due to heat of 212°F (100°C)
bombardier	bom′ buh dir′	one who operates bomb-sights
Bomby	bom′ bē	proper name—short for bom-bardier
Brachinus	brok′ uhn uhs	family of beetles
business	biz′ nis	work—occupation
calosoma	kal uh sō′ muh	a branch of the beetle family
canals	kuh nal′z	artifical waterway
cannon	kan′ uhn	large gun
carabid	kar′ uh bid	ground beetle
carbine	kär′ bīn	short, light rifle
catalase	kat′ uh lāz	chemical that changes a substance without itself being changed
cataloged	cat′ uh logd	arrange and list in order
cell	sel	the tiniest living part of things
celsius	sel′ sē uhs	scale used in centigrade ther-mometer; 0° = freez-ing—100° = boiling
chamber	chām′ br̀	a room in a house
charge	chär′j	rush forward with force
chemicals	kem′ uh kuhlz	made or used in chemistry

Glossary

chew	chü	crush or grind with teeth
children	chil′druhn	boys and girls; offspring
continued	kuhn tin′ūd	keep on and on
corner	kôr′nuhr	place where lines meet
countries	kun′trēz	lands, regions
cousin	kuz′uhn	son or daughter of your aunt or uncle
Creator	krē′ā′tuhr	one who makes
creatures	krē′chuhrz	living beings
danger	dān′juhr	chance of harm
Diery	dir′ē	proper name
dozing	dōz′ing	napping
dragons	drag′uhnz	huge snakelike animals
earth	èrth	planet upon which we live
elytra	el′uh truh	more than one elytron
elytron	el′uh tron	either of a pair of thickened front wings
enemies	en′uh mēz	person or group that hates another
English	ing′glish	having to do with England
environment	in vī′ruhn mint	things or conditions where you live that affect you
evening	ēv′ning	latter part of the day
exhaust	ig zôst′	to empty, drain
explain	ik splān′	to tell how to do
explodes	ik splōd′z	to blow up
extinct	ik stingkt′	no longer living or being
entomologist	in tō môl′uh jist	a person who studies insects
Fahrenheit	far′uhn hīt	scale for measuring temperature; 32° = freezing—212° = boiling
fierce	firs	wild, raging
friends	frendz	person who knows and likes another
fossil	fôs′suhl	remains of a plant or animal found in earth or rock

38

Glossary

genus	jē′ nuhs	kind of or related animals or plants
glands	glandz	an organ of the body
grew	grü	get bigger (past tense)
howled	hould	long, loud, sad cry
huge	hüj	extremely large in size
hydrogen	hī′ druh juhn	light colorless gas
hydroquinone	hī drō kwi nōn′	white sweetish compound
insect	in′ sekt	any member of a class of tiny winged animals having no back bone (invertebrate)
juice	jüs	liquid part of fruit
knights	nīts	soldier who wears armor
learn	lèrn	to gain knowledge
listen	lis′ uhn	to try to hear, pay attention
machine	muh shēn′	device for applying power and doing work
members	mem′ buhrz	belonging to a group
munching	munch′ ing	chew with vigor
nectar	nek′ tuhr	sweet liquid from flowers
once	wuns	one time only
orb	ôrb	sphere, globe
peroxidase	puh räk′ suh dās	enzyme found in many plants
peroxide	puh räk′ sīd	oxide containing oxygen
petrified	pet′ ruh fīd	turn to stone
plank	plank	long flat sawed timber about 2″ thick
poison	poi′ zuhn	drug dangerous to life

Glossary

pretend	pri tend′	to claim falsely
protection	prō tek′ shuhn	to keep from harm
protein	prō′ tēn	compound necessary to life of plants and animals
pupa	pü′ puh	stage of insect between larva and adult
questions	kwes′ chuhnz	to ask, inquire
resin	rez′ uhn	sap of trees, especially pine or fir
responsibilities	ri spon′ suh bil′ uh tēz	tasks, jobs to do
scare	skār	to frighten
scientific	sī uhn tif′ ik	according to laws of science
smithereens	smith′ uh rēnz′	(informal) small bits or pieces
solution	suh lü′ shuhn	solve a problem, explanation
specialist	spesh′ uh list	person who works in one branch of study
species	spē′ sēz	a class of animals
spider	spī′ duhr	little eight-legged creature
staggered	stag′ uhrd	sway from side to side
story	stôr′ ē	an account of a happening
stories	stôr′ ēz	more than one story
system	sis′ tuhm	set of things making a whole.
teach	tēch	give knowledge
threads	thredz	small cords
tiger	tī′ guhr	large fierce cat
tiny	tī′ nē	very small
urged	èrjd	drive onward, push
valves	valvz	movable part to control flow of liquid or gas, faucet